DEATH ROLLS IN

A SEASONED SLEUTH COZY MYSTERY, BOOK 1

GRETCHEN ALLEN

SUMMER PRESCOTT BOOKS PUBLISHING

Copyright 2023 Summer Prescott Books

All Rights Reserved. No part of this publication nor any of the information herein may be quoted from, nor reproduced, in any form, including but not limited to: printing, scanning, photocopying, or any other printed, digital, or audio formats, without prior express written consent of the copyright holder.

**This book is a work of fiction. Any similarities to persons, living or dead, places of business, or situations past or present, is completely unintentional.

CHAPTER ONE

"There isn't a thing about this place that makes me happy to be here." Clarence Barksdale sat on the tailgate of his pickup truck and watched the small ripples in the clear, blue lake lap the shore. He straightened the trucker cap on his head and reached for another box to hand off to his sister.

"Then it's a good thing you're not the one moving here," Loretta said to him. She tucked the box under her arm, grabbed the small lamp she intended to keep on her bedside table, and headed inside without a look back.

"Why are you so excited about moving into an old trailer, anyway?" Clarence called after her.

"Just unload the rest of the boxes," Loretta muttered. She walked through the small garage and up a couple of steps into the kitchen to put her things down. He'd just said it to get under her skin. In truth, her new house was a modular home, even if it was more than thirty years old.

"You know, when you told me you bought a place to retire in Florida, this was not what I pictured." Clarence dropped the last pair of small boxes on the wide kitchen island and leaned against the refrigerator.

"What did you expect?" Loretta asked. She did her best to plaster on a patient smile. "You know as well as anybody what I am able to afford and what I am not. Besides, if you don't want to be here helping me move in, you don't have to be."

"Yes, I do," Clarence said. "Who else is going to help you out? You said it yourself on the way here. You're all alone in the world, aside from me."

"Thank you for the reminder, dear brother," Loretta said. She snatched up the lamp and headed to the small bedroom where her queen-size bed and two small side tables had already been set up. She placed the lamp on one of the tables and sat down hard on the bare mattress.

"Hey, look, Lor," Clarence said from the doorway. "I'm just tired and out of sorts, that's all. I think it's a nice little area, all things considered. You've got that big old lake and a bunch of nice trees surrounding the trailers. I, um, mean, the houses."

Loretta jutted her chin out defiantly, despite the tears that stung her eyes. "It's the one place I found that checks all of my boxes. It's affordable. It's located close to water and far away from Herring Heights. Oh, and the weather is promising."

"Unless it's hurricane season," Clarence quipped.

"Seriously? A little support here would be nice," Loretta said. She hung her head.

"I am supportive." Clarence crossed the floor and took a seat next to her on the bed. "Would I have traveled this far with you if I wasn't supportive?"

Loretta shook her head. "You never turn down a chance to get away from Susie," she said. She turned to her younger brother. "You told me yourself that you should pay me for giving you the chance to get away from your wife for the weekend."

"I did say that, didn't I?" He chuckled. "It's the truth, but I did come to help you out. You've been through enough."

Loretta cleared her throat and stood up abruptly. She was finished with the pity party and wanted to complete the moving process as fast as possible. "Which is precisely why this retirement community is the perfect answer."

"Retirement community." Clarence huffed and shook his head. He folded his hands and leaned forward on his elbows. "You're far too young to move to a retirement community. You barely qualified for the age restrictions, for crying out loud. You're still young and vibrant, and you know it as well as I do."

"Clarence, I don't want to go over all of that again," Loretta said. "You know my reasons for moving to a place like this."

"I understand the reasons you think you have," he said. "But I think you're acting hastily."

"Again, you're not the one moving here," Loretta mumbled under her breath. She walked out of the bedroom and back through the large living room area. Like most of the homes along Breezy Lake, picture windows covered the back of the house facing the lake, and smaller windows lined the front.

It was through one of those front windows that Loretta spotted a short, round woman with wild reddish hair, heading straight up to her house. She was shocked when she heard the kitchen door open. "Hello," a voice called out. Loretta rounded the corner into the kitchen and stood almost face to face with the stranger. She looked down when a high-pitched yip filled the room.

"You have a dog," Loretta said.

"Oh, yes," the woman said. She smiled the smile of an indulgent mother and bent down to pat the mess of hair and teeth at the other end of the leash she held in her hand. "You will come to find out that Mr. Nigel here is a bit of a mascot around Breezy Lake."

"Who are you, exactly?" Loretta asked. She forced herself to maintain a light tone of voice. She stared at the woman, whom she could only describe as bouncy. Her entire body vibrated as she spoke, which was a spectacle in itself given the way she was dressed. Her legs were covered in skintight black leggings, and she wore a long, oversized tunic in wild colors. Her pinkish-red hair was gathered behind an orange scarf tied in a bow on the top of her head. Loretta watched in disbelief as even the hair on top of her head flounced with each word the woman spoke.

"Oh, someone should have already told you about me. My name is Pauline Pendleton," the woman said. "I'm shocked to find out they didn't tell you who I was when you bought this property. Anyway, I suppose you've already been told about the clubs here. You do know you have to join a club of some sort, right? Well, I can tell you, my club is the most popular for newcomers. We're the Clubhouse Cooks and it's exactly what it sounds like. We're a group of people, ladies mostly, who put together large community meals at least once per month in the clubhouse on the other side of the lake. You need to appear before the committee before they'll let you into the club, but for me, the committee was simply a formality. Everyone around here considers me the unofficial mayor, anyway. You'll have to impress me more than you'll need to worry about impressing all of them."

Pauline Pendleton spoke longer than Loretta had ever seen another human being speak without pausing for at least one breath. She stared at her, only able to think about how, right now, the Clubhouse Cooks sounded like the last club she'd ever want to join, despite her great love for cooking.

Clarence appeared from the hallway and stood against the doorway into the living room with his arms folded. Pauline looked him up and down and screwed up her face in clear disapproval. "Who are you?" she snapped. "I didn't get a notice about two people moving in here."

"I'm the poor soul who had to listen to you yammer on for five straight minutes," Clarence shot back. "Who the heck are you supposed to be? The welcome wagon?"

Nigel, the Pomeranian, growled, interrupting whatever argument was about to occur. Loretta watched as the first meeting with anyone from her new neighborhood dissolved into a disaster before her eyes. She didn't have time to scold her brother for being rude, as she had forgotten to account for Milo. The high-pitched shrill of the large cat's meow reminded her.

"Oh, no!" Loretta shouted just as the oversized tuxedo cat emerged from his place in the laundry room. He took a flying leap toward the Pomeranian. His paws were spread wide, and his claws were extended for maximum damage. The small dog saw his end coming and promptly yelped and ran through the house, ripping his leash from his owner's hand.

"Milo," Clarence commanded from the doorway. Loretta watched as the cat looked up, midflight, not at all caring about what trouble he'd started. Unfortunately, no human being was able to stop a cat on a mission. Somehow, her seventeen-pound furball had managed to change its direction and begin his chase. Poor Nigel didn't stand a chance.

It was all too much for Pauline, who screamed each time the animals raced past her. Eventually, Clarence was able to capture a fearful Nigel. Milo skidded to a halt and casually sauntered back toward the laundry room as though he hadn't just caused the dog's life to flash before its eyes.

"What was that thing?" Pauline demanded with

exaggerated horror. "Some sort of miniature werewolf?"

"That's just Milo," Clarence volunteered. "He's my sister's watch cat. With him around, there's no need for a dog."

"We don't allow animals in this community," Pauline snapped. "You will have to get rid of him right away."

"No one said anything about no animals allowed." Loretta felt her heart sink in her chest. Milo might be a sight to behold, but he was family to her. The only family she was going to have in her new home.

"Nonsense, lady." Clarence stepped in front of the other woman and leaned against the kitchen island beside his sister. "You have a dog."

"Well, the rules are different for some people who have been here a long time," Pauline said quickly.

"That's not quite right," Clarence continued. "If I remember correctly, according to the bylaws here, once the house has been purchased, nobody can tell you that you aren't allowed to have a pet. As long as it's not an illegally kept animal, there isn't a thing you can say about it."

She rolled her eyes. "What are you, some kind of wannabe lawyer or something?"

"As a matter of fact, I happen to be an attorney,"

Clarence said with a broad grin. "And I will make sure no one runs over my sister with ridiculous notions."

"Well, I can tell that you are not going to be a good fit for this community," Pauline said. She pulled upward on Nigel's leash and steered him toward the kitchen door.

"Then I suppose it's a good thing I'm only visiting. Oh, and by the way, most people wait until they are invited to walk into someone's house before they just help themselves," Clarence called after her.

Loretta shook her head and walked behind Pauline to the door. "I hope we can get along despite this rough introduction," she said. "I've spent everything I have on this place, Mrs. Pendleton. I'm your neighbor now, for better or for worse." She chuckled slightly, hoping to release some of the tension.

Pauline whipped her head around. "We'll have to see about that," she hissed. She glared at Loretta over the frame of her colorful glasses. "You see, nobody remains at Breezy Lake for long if I don't approve of them, and I surely don't approve of you or your beast of a cat." She yanked on the leash, and Nigel scrambled to catch up with her as she walked back down the driveway.

"Sorry," Clarence said. "I didn't mean to cause you any trouble."

"It's okay," Loretta sighed. "I have a feeling that trouble would have found me whether you spoke up or not."

CHAPTER TWO

"Tell us a little about yourself," the man seated at the head of the table said to Loretta the following morning. She stood at a podium in front of a table with five strangers sitting behind it.

Her first night at Breezy Lake Village had gone by without incident, despite her irreverent introduction to the self-proclaimed unofficial mayor of the village, Pauline Pendleton. Once Clarence left, Loretta made the decision to appear before the Clubhouse Cooks committee, after all.

"Well, I'm from Herring Heights, New Hampshire," Loretta began. She felt her hands shaking slightly. Speaking in front of large groups didn't usually bother her, but this particular situation felt different.

"What sort of culinary experience do you have?" the man asked her. She read the nameplate in front of him. Wally Neville. He was a tall man with a full head of salt and pepper hair, and his dark eyes appeared kind when he spoke. Loretta vaguely remembered seeing his wife Gwen's name on the welcome packet she'd received when she bought the house.

"I owned a bistro in town for twenty years," Loretta said. "I designed the menu and ran every part of the place until it closed a year ago."

"Why did it close?" one of the women on the panel asked. Brigitte Waldorf was the name on the plate in front of her.

"I sold it to my business partner," Loretta said with a forced smile. Her answer wasn't a total lie. She had purchased her home at Breezy Lake Village from the money Martin had given her after he forced her out. The rest of the story was no one's business, least of all a group of self-important retirees sitting in front of her judging whether or not her culinary expertise was good enough for their so-called Clubhouse Cooks.

"It sure sounds like there's more to that story. What else will you be sharing with us?" Brigitte pressed.

DEATH ROLLS IN   13

"Ms. Barksdale is under no obligation to divulge her life's story for our benefit," Nina Carpenter said. She was a dark-haired woman seated next to Brigitte. She appeared poised and not easily rattled. Loretta liked her instantly. "I would like to know a little bit about your favorite dishes."

Loretta nodded. "That's simple enough. I prepare a scrumptious chicken pot pie with a flaky, buttery crust draped over the top. My favorite accompaniment is a simple green salad and hard, crusty rolls."

"What dressing would you use for the salad?" Nina asked.

"My locally famous poppyseed vinaigrette," Loretta said. Her brain seemed to fire on all cylinders. "It's sweet and tangy and great over spinach and strawberries."

Wally smiled and nodded toward Nina. "I think we should take this to a vote," he said. "I'm thoroughly convinced already. I vote yes."

"Same with me," Nina said.

Two more members nodded their heads affirmatively. Only Brigitte shook her head. "I don't think we know enough about her," she mumbled, loud enough for everyone else to hear.

"Brigitte, we never know anyone until they've been here awhile." Wally chuckled. He pushed back from the table and stood up. Brigitte followed suit then made her way straight for Pauline, who was seated at the far end of the back row of chairs.

Loretta smiled at several of the members and headed toward the door of the clubhouse. Her home was on the opposite side of the lake, and she planned on a few hours of solitude before making any more efforts to get to know her neighbors. On one of her last shopping excursions in Herring Heights, Loretta had picked up a new historical novel to enjoy after she settled in. There was nothing more pressing in her world at that moment than a date with her novel and a cup of coffee under a shady tree by the lake.

She walked past the rows of chairs toward the exit and felt a sudden tug on her arm. She turned to face Brigitte and Pauline. Both women stood with their hands planted on their hips, staring expectantly at her.

"Hello, ladies. Can I help you?" Loretta asked.

"You bet you can," Pauline said. She folded her arms over her chest and stared hard at Loretta.

"Okay, and how can I help you?" She felt a twinge of annoyance, a warning to her that she needed to find a quiet spot to sit and regroup for a while. There was no need for her to let her emotions get the best of her.

"Well," Pauline huffed. "Since you nosed your

way into the Clubhouse Cooks, I don't think it's right for you to leave until you've been given your first assignment."

She'd hardly nosed her way in. It was Pauline herself who had told her about the club in the first place, but Loretta decided to overlook that for the moment. "Okay, and what will my assignment be?" Loretta asked patiently. She was prepared to spend part of the day in the kitchen, whipping up one of her favorite dishes from her days as the owner of a bistro.

Pauline smiled at her. For a moment, she reminded Loretta of the Cheshire Cat from Alice in Wonderland. "We have a dinner planned for tomorrow night, and since you're the new kid in town, we need someone to prepare enough dinner rolls for two hundred people."

"Two hundred! You want me to prepare enough bread for that many people?"

"Oh, yes," Brigitte said. She cast a smirk at Pauline and continued, "We also need five cakes for dessert and a few gallons of punch for the refreshment table."

Loretta blinked twice and shook her head. "You want me to do all of that?"

"Are you incapable of getting that done?" Brigitte asked. She raised her eyebrows in mock concern.

"Surely someone with your background and expertise should be able to handle that without a problem."

"I think it's a bit much to expect a single person to provide rolls for two hundred people, plus five cakes, and several gallons of punch in less than a day's time," Loretta shot back. "I'm sure I can make it happen, but I still think it's an excessive ask."

Nina approached the women from behind. "What's going on over here?"

"We were just giving our new Clubhouse Cooks member her first assignment," Brigitte said.

"From what I heard, you're attempting to give her enough assignments for a small army," Nina said. She turned to Loretta. "If you'd like to prepare some dinner rolls for tomorrow night, we would be most grateful. You'll find a key code for the door to this building in the packet of papers you were provided at the end of the meeting. Feel free to come and go as you please. Utilize the freezers and other spaces as needed, too."

"That's very kind of you, but I didn't receive any packet after the meeting," Loretta said. She noticed Brigitte's eyes narrowing as she spoke.

Nina frowned. "That's something one of our committee members was supposed to get to you. I'm sure Brigitte forgot with all the excitement of bringing in a new club member. We'll wait right here while she runs back to her table to grab it." She turned her attention back to Loretta. "Is that something you can do? The rolls, I mean."

Loretta smiled. She said nothing to Brigitte when she returned and roughly handed over the white envelope filled with papers.

"Yes, I'll be happy to make some dinner rolls for tomorrow. I'll bring as many as I can, and hopefully, they will be a great example of my culinary capabilities. I look forward to offering more items as time goes on." She said her goodbyes and turned toward the door, thankful to be heading back home.

CHAPTER THREE

"Oh, good grief." Loretta stopped dead in her tracks. Her arms ached under the weight of the tray she balanced in her arms. She stood in the clubhouse doorway and stared at the lumpy figure on the floor in the middle of the darkened room before her. The only light coming into the room was at her back. Her hands were too full to flip on the lights on the wall five feet away.

She was staring at something that appeared entirely out of place. Loretta looked down at the dozens of homemade rolls on the tray in her arms. "If I could just set these down," she mumbled to herself and turned to the table closest to her. She carefully placed the tray on top of the table and rushed over to the wall and began hitting switches. The room instantly filled with light.

Loretta turned around and walked through a pair of tables to get a closer look. At first, the lump looked like a pair of discarded black trash bags, but upon closer inspection, her worst fear was confirmed. It was a person, though exactly who was not immediately apparent to her. She wasn't sure of age or gender, either. Whoever it was, was dressed in a pair of loose-fitting sweatpants and a dark-colored sweatshirt. The hood was pulled up over the head, hiding the face. The only body part she could see was the back of a hand.

She turned away out of respect, quite sure of the state of the body given the bluish tint of the skin, and instinctively reached for her cell phone. She cursed herself for leaving it on the counter at home and rushed back out the door. "Help!" she called out. A few people stood outside, but they were too far away to hear her. "Help!" she called louder and waved her hand over her head.

"What's the matter with you?" Loretta turned to the plump woman heading toward her. She closed her eyes for a moment and begged the universe to replace the woman rushing at her with anyone else on the planet. The clown from her favorite Stephen King novel came to mind as someone she would rather face.

Instead, Pauline Pendleton raced forward, pulling Nigel the Pomeranian behind her. Her pinkish-red hair piled high on the top of her head flounced as she walked. "I knew you were here to wreck things."

"Wreck things? What are you talking about?" Loretta asked. She wasn't the least bit concerned about hiding her true feelings at the moment.

"I'm talking about the fact that you only just moved into this community and you're already standing outside the clubhouse in the middle of the night shouting for help," Pauline said.

"It's hardly the middle of the night," Loretta countered, knowing it was barely after six o'clock. "I'm calling out for help because I think there's someone dead in the middle of the clubhouse. I forgot my cellphone at home."

"What were you doing in there?" Pauline scoffed.

"You know darn good and well what I'm doing," Loretta replied. "You do recall the Clubhouse Cooks meeting we were both present at earlier today, right?"

"Yes, I recall the meeting." Pauline swiped at the air with her well-manicured hand. "There's nothing wrong with my memory."

Loretta nodded. "Then you know the committee

asked me to supply dinner rolls for tomorrow night. I had to get an early start on them in order to make enough. I was just here to bring the first batch over so there was less to carry at once."

"That doesn't explain why you're standing out here shouting like a banshee," Pauline said. "Besides, the committee was only doing you a favor by asking you to make the dinner rolls. I'm the one who calls the shots around here. Don't you forget that."

"Pauline, I don't care one bit about who is in charge or who isn't," Loretta said. "There's a dead body inside the clubhouse. We need to get the cops over here as soon as possible."

"Oh, you're just a mess," Pauline said. She pushed past Loretta and headed for the door to the clubhouse. She shoved the leash into Loretta's hand as she walked past her. Nigel circled around her ankles and began nipping at her pants.

"I don't like dogs," Loretta called after Pauline.

"Just hang onto Nigel while I check things out in here," Pauline called back. Loretta heard the clatter of several metal folding chairs as Pauline moved through the room. She stepped carefully out of the tangled leash Nigel had wrapped around her feet and pulled the growling dog behind her toward the building.

"I don't need you to check things out," Loretta

said through the open door. "I need you to call the police."

Pauline walked over to the body and cast an irritated glare back toward Loretta. She slowly knelt down and sighed impatiently. "Oh my gosh!" She screamed and fell backward on her round bottom. She turned toward Loretta, her eyes wild with concern. "Do you know what that is?"

"As I told you outside, it is a dead body," Loretta said calmly. She held the leash steady despite Nigel turning his small, sharp teeth to her ankles. "Now, will you please either call the police or point me to a phone so I can do it myself?"

CHAPTER FOUR

There was a flurry of activity all around. Loretta could see several people from the community forming a circle around the front of the building. Her eyes moved to the shimmering lake behind them. She wanted nothing more than to return to the comfortable chair under the tree in the back of her house, but here she was, just a few days after moving to her new home, dealing with the police.

Her plan to spend the rest of her life in affordable solitude was off to a bad start. She had no idea who was inside the building in the middle of the clubhouse floor. All she knew was that her choice of a retirement community suddenly seemed like one of the worst decisions she had ever made, aside, of course, from her marriage to Martin Ashcroft.

Martin was the reason she'd found herself in the dire financial straits that had sent her looking for paradise at a bargain-basement price in the first place. Clarence had been right about him. Her ex-husband was bad news, and as soon as she'd learned that for herself, she made plans to move somewhere warm and easy on her body. At just fifty years old, she was hard pressed to find a community she qualified to reside in. Breezy Lake Village was a good fit, minus the situation she'd found herself in. It was near the water, affordable, easy to navigate, and located in Florida where the weather year-round was temperate. A decent change from the cold, New England winters.

"Loretta Barksdale, correct?" A gruff-voiced sheriff's deputy stood in front of her. He hunched over a tablet of paper and scrawled notes.

"That's right," she said. "I just moved into the community."

The deputy peered up at her over his metal-framed glasses. "You're the one who found the victim?"

"The victim." Loretta let out a heavy breath. The word took her off guard. She hadn't considered that the person inside the clubhouse was a victim of a crime. Victim meant murder, and until that moment, it had not dawned on Loretta that she had just happened upon an actual crime.

"Yes, the victim." The deputy surveyed her. "You are the one who discovered the body of Nina Carpenter?"

"Nina?" Loretta's hand went straight to her mouth. She had just met the woman earlier in the day. "She's the one inside there? What happened to her?"

"I was hoping you might be able to shed some light on that for me," he said.

Loretta searched the deputy's face. He was easily over forty, possibly closer to fifty. His mouth was framed in a gray goatee. She could see tufts of salt and pepper hair poking out from underneath his hat. She spotted a name tag on his uniform. "H. Hargraves" was engraved on the gold-colored tag next to the symbol for the sheriff's department.

"I don't know what you mean, Deputy Hargraves," Loretta said. "I came in here with a tray of rolls for the dinner tomorrow night. I set the tray down as soon as I spotted the lump in the middle of the room."

"Then what happened?" Deputy Hargraves asked.

"I went outside," she said. "I realized I didn't have my phone with me, so I ran outside to call for help. Pauline was out walking her dog, and she was the first person I came across."

"How well did you know the victim?" he asked her.

Loretta shook her head. "I had only just met her. She's on the Clubhouse Cooks committee, and I appeared before them this morning, hoping to join their club. Nina was very nice to me. She's the one who made sure I had access to the building."

"If this dinner isn't until tomorrow, why were you here tonight?" Deputy Hargraves asked.

"Because the number of rolls needed for the dinner is quite high," Loretta said. "I decided to get a head start on baking."

"Did it anger you that she asked you to do so much?" Deputy Hargraves asked.

"What? No! Of course not." Loretta felt the frustration well up inside her. Her legs weakened, and she stumbled backward slightly. "I had no reason to feel anything negative toward the woman at all. Aside from the few moments I spoke with her at the committee meeting, I had never met the woman before in my life. She wasn't even the one who asked me to make the rolls to begin with."

"Ma'am, are you intoxicated?" Deputy Hargraves

took a step toward her. Loretta heard him call out her name a few more times, until his voice sounded distant and tinny, and she felt the earth draw closer to her.

CHAPTER FIVE

"They think you had too much to drink." Loretta turned her head in the direction of the voice. She could hear unfamiliar beeps and tones in the distance. She blinked her eyes open and stared at the woman sitting beside her. Shocks of pinkish-red hair stood up all over the woman's head.

"What do you want, Pauline?" Loretta groaned. She closed her eyes. Her head was pounding, and her side hurt.

"You fell down," Pauline announced. "There wasn't anybody else to go to the hospital with you, so I rode along. Nobody else here knows a thing about you."

"Where am I?" Loretta asked. Her eyes flew open. She was in a bed, presumably a hospital bed.

"Lakeview General Hospital," Pauline said. Loretta studied the other woman's face. She expected a sneer or a smirk, but there was something else in her countenance. "You passed out. Did you have a few drinks while you were baking?"

"No." Loretta shook her head. "I don't drink."

"Well, I don't mean to pry," Pauline said. Her mannerisms had shifted slightly. Loretta wondered if there was something more going on that somehow brought out a softer side of the older woman. "But the deputy back there was pretty sure you were under the influence when talking to him."

"Then hopefully the hospital performed a blood test that would prove otherwise," Loretta said. She leaned forward when a nurse entered the room. She glanced at Pauline, hopeful she would get the clue.

Instead, Pauline stood up with her hands on her hips. Loretta thought the hands-on-hips position was probably Pauline's default look. "What can you tell us, Nurse?"

"I would prefer to discuss my medical information in private," Loretta said firmly. She turned and looked at Pauline, then cleared her throat.

"Yes, that's reasonable." The nurse gazed at Pauline and waited. "Madam, I am going to ask you to step out in the hall while I speak with the patient alone."

"Oh, you want me to leave?" Pauline raised her eyebrows.

"I would like some privacy, if you don't mind," Loretta said calmly.

"Fine," Pauline said, doubtful there was a question about her place in the room. "I'll be right outside if you need me."

"Thank you." Loretta smiled slightly as Pauline reluctantly left the room. She felt a slight spike of concern when she spotted the uniformed police officer posted outside of her hospital room through the open door.

"Some friend you have there," the nurse said.

"She's not really my friend," Loretta said. "I just moved into a new house, and she lives in the same area."

"Breezy Lake," the nurse mused. "My aunt lived out there for a while."

"She doesn't now?" Loretta asked. A second later, she hoped the aunt hadn't passed away. Her words might have been a little premature.

The nurse shook her head. "Let's just say that she decided the ladies in the neighborhood were a little too much. If your friend is any indication, I think she chose wisely."

Loretta chuckled. "Suppose we get down to the brass tacks," she said. "What's going on with me?"

"Let me start by introducing myself. My name is Maisy, and I'm a nurse practitioner here at the hospital. I've gone over your chart, and I think you simply experienced an unfortunate, high-stress situation that caused you to faint. All your tests have come back just fine other than low blood pressure, but tell me, have you established a doctor here?"

"Not yet," Loretta said. She grimaced slightly. "My move here was rather abrupt."

"I can recommend a few names if you'd like," Maisy said. "Your tests may have come back okay, but it's important that you take care of yourself."

Loretta nodded. "Sure, I'll take some names, but really, I think it was like you said before; a high-stress situation. Then with the move and all, I guess I just haven't been drinking enough water or getting enough sleep. I promise I'll do better."

"Good. If you're interested, you can probably start with the practice where I work three days a week. I'm almost certain we're accepting new patients." She passed a business card to Loretta and stood up again.

"Thanks, Maisy. Are you sure everything is okay with me?"

"You're going to be fine. You can cook and bake and take walks and even go dancing if you want. Just increase your fluids and stay away from any dead bodies if you can help it." She helped Loretta back up off of the bed and placed her hand on her arm.

Loretta chuckled slightly and straightened her clothing. She waited while the nurse left the room, and Pauline filed back in as quickly as she could.

CHAPTER SIX

"I knew it," she said. "You're dying, aren't you?"

"I am not dying," Loretta said quietly. She glanced up at the officer waiting in the hallway. "I have low blood pressure, and I tend not to handle stressful situations all that well. I never used to be like this, but here we are. Life has finally started to catch up to me, I'm afraid."

"What is it? Cancer? Lupus? Halitosis?" Pauline's eyes were wide with concern.

"Halitosis? You mean bad breath?" Loretta asked.

"Well, you don't have to correct me all the time," Pauline said. "Just tell me. Are you dying?"

"Pauline, I told you already. I'm not dying, and I hope you will forgive me that I don't want to share more about my life with you just yet."

"Yes, I suppose that's okay." Pauline nodded. "Well, let's get you home."

Loretta stared at the loud hair on the back of the woman's head as she followed behind her.

"Where are you going?" the police officer barked as they walked past him.

"Home, I think," Loretta said. "I was released from care. Is there a reason I can't leave?"

The officer shook his head and frowned. "The sheriff's department asked us to keep an eye out for you ladies while you're in here. I guess there is some concern over your safety."

Loretta smiled slightly and nodded to the officer. "Well, we're going home now."

Pauline nodded and hooked her arm in Loretta's, then headed down the hall toward the exit. She led her through the parking lot without a word, then to her baby blue Oldsmobile Delta 88. She opened the passenger door for Loretta and practically shoved her inside.

Pauline drove for thirty minutes without saying a single word. Loretta wondered if there was an identical twin that answered to the name of Pauline Pendleton as well. She couldn't believe that the woman with the loud hair and the evil dog was driving quietly back to their homes in Breezy Lake Village.

Brigitte Waldorf greeted the car as soon as Pauline pulled off the county highway and into the entrance of the retirement community. She tapped loudly on the driver's window and motioned for Pauline to roll it down.

"What are you doing?" Brigitte asked. "Why is she with you?"

"I gave her a ride home from the hospital," Pauline said. The shrill nature of her voice had waned. "Just move out of the way and let me get out of this car."

"Thank you for the ride," Loretta said. "I can walk from here."

"Yeah, you're welcome," Pauline muttered. She slammed her car door behind her and took off somewhere with Brigitte. The moon shone over the lake. Bright lights burned overhead, illuminating the parking lot and the narrow road into the neighborhood.

Loretta spotted the large community building on the other side of the lake. She began the long walk alone toward her house, passing a number of people as she walked. A few looked up at her with mild curiosity. One or two offered a weak smile. She spotted a woman with flaxen-blonde hair cut to her chin. The woman smiled broadly and walked toward her.

"Are you Loretta?" the woman asked. "I'm Gwen Neville, Wally's wife. I understand you've had quite a night."

"Nice to meet you, Gwen," Loretta said. "I'm sorry if I'm not very sociable right now."

"It's understandable," Gwen said. "Would you like some company while you walk? I could use some fresh air myself. As you can imagine, everything is quite a mess around here. Everyone is wondering who could have put their hands on Nina Carpenter. Of all people, why Nina?" Gwen shook her head sadly as she walked.

"I didn't know her for very long, but she seemed like a nice human being," Loretta said. "How long did you know her?"

"Oh, how long," Gwen breathed. "Well, Wally and I moved here ten years ago. I think Nina was here a year or two later."

Loretta nodded as she walked along slowly. Her feet and legs felt heavy. Although it was just before nine, she yearned for a good night's rest in her own bed. To her surprise, there was no sign of the deputy she had met earlier.

"Her death doesn't make any sense," Loretta said. She continued the conversation with the woman who was kind enough to walk her home. "I had only just met her at the committee meeting, but she seemed like a good, fair woman."

"She was that indeed," Gwen said. "She was that and a lot of other things, actually. I just don't understand who would have had so much rage in their hearts. It must have taken a lot to gather up the courage to hit her that hard. Some people can be so cruel."

"Do you know if there was anyone who might wish her harm?" Loretta asked. "I think Deputy Hargraves questioned me for a little while just because I'm the new face around here."

Gwen chuckled. "Sometimes it isn't a good thing to be the new kid in town," she said.

"It's been quite a long time since anyone referred to me as a kid." Loretta laughed.

"Oh, hush," Gwen said. "Compared to the rest of us, you're a teenager. Can I be bold and ask just how old you are? There's hardly any gray in your hair! You don't look a day over forty."

Loretta grinned. The words hit her ego just the right way. "I turned fifty two months ago."

"So, you barely qualified to live here," Gwen said.

"I'm not sure, but you might be the youngest resident we've ever had."

"This was the only fifty-plus community I found," Loretta said. "Most of the other retirement communities only allow people over fifty-five."

"Not to mention the fact that this is one of the most affordable communities in the state of Florida," Gwen said.

"That was another reason I chose Breezy Lake," Loretta said.

"I didn't see a husband on your paperwork," Gwen said. "I'm not trying to pry, but as young as you are, it's rather unusual that you came alone."

The conversation had gone into uncomfortable territory for Loretta. She inhaled deeply. She knew the questions would come one way or another. Perhaps it was best that she gave out enough information to satiate curiosity from the get-go, and maybe the calmer, kinder woman next to her was the best person to confide in. Controlled information, Loretta thought.

"Divorce," she said. "Last year."

"Oh, divorce." Gwen smiled but seemed to catch herself. She shook her head slowly. "I'm not sure which is worse, death or divorce."

"Sometimes one makes you wish for the other,"

Loretta said ruefully. "I'll let you guess which one is which."

"I take it the split was not an amicable one," Gwen said. She turned her body slightly and held up both of her hands. "I don't mean to pry."

"Yes, you do, a little," Loretta teased.

"Okay, guilty," Gwen admitted. "We don't get too many new faces around here, and when we do, Pauline and Brigitte usually get to them before the rest of us can ask questions."

"It's normal, I suppose," Loretta said. "I guess I would want to know as well. To answer your question, the split was not a happy one. I decided a move to another side of the country was in order after the divorce."

"Well, as much as I want to question whether he had a woman on the side, I will restrain my curiosity," Gwen said. She stopped walking in front of Loretta's driveway. "For now, anyway. Maybe we can become friends and you might trust me enough to tell me the rest of the story."

Loretta nodded. "Maybe." She had the feeling that the two of them might be friends in time. "I really am quite a boring person. You haven't told me a thing about yourself yet."

"No, I haven't," Gwen said with a grin. She

turned to walk back toward the main entrance. "I suppose we'll have to meet up for coffee sometime and discuss that."

"Sounds good." Loretta waved slightly and headed inside.

Milo met her at the front door, meowing loudly at her as she walked. "What's the matter, big guy?" Loretta asked.

She reached down to pet his head. Milo responded with a hiss and a prominent view of his backside.

"Fine. I get it. You're mad at me."

She walked across the living room and into the kitchen. She half expected to find evidence of the large feline's anger on the floor as she walked. The kitchen floor was clean, but the floor of the laundry room appeared as if a kitty litter bomb had exploded on the floor.

"Really, Milo?" She rolled her eyes at the cat and pulled the broom off the rack behind the door.

CHAPTER SEVEN

Loretta woke to her cat growling above her early the next morning. She opened her eyes to find Milo standing at the top of her bed. His large head was not visible to her. He had pushed it between the mini blinds and the window looking over the lake behind her house.

"What is the matter with you, Milo?" Loretta asked. She pushed her hair away from her face and grabbed her glasses off the nightstand next to her bed. She sat up slightly and opened a small section of the blinds to peer outside.

"Seriously?" Loretta grabbed the bathrobe off the hook behind her bathroom door and headed down the hall to the kitchen. She opened the door to the back deck and sighed. "Nigel! Stop digging holes in my yard!"

"Why are you yelling at my dog?" Pauline called out. Loretta looked around the yard for signs of the woman.

"Where are you?" Loretta asked.

"Out here on the road," she called back. "Where do you think I am?"

Loretta walked to the far end of the deck and peered around the side of the house. She spotted Pauline on the road, dressed in a fuzzy pink and purple bathrobe and slippers. Loretta looked down at her ivory-colored robe and bit the inside of her cheek to prevent the words bubbling up inside her from coming out.

"Why is your dog digging to the ends of the earth in my backyard?" Loretta asked. "And why are you out there while he's doing it?"

"Well, because I don't want to trespass on your property," Pauline said. Her hand went straight to her hip. "We take private property quite seriously around here."

"Obviously," Loretta muttered.

"What was that?" Pauline called out.

"Never mind," Loretta said. "I just wish your dog could choose a better place to tear things up."

"Where do you expect him to do it?" Pauline shouted. "In my yard? You really are a different duck, Loretta Barksdale." She whistled for the dog to join her. Loretta watched with amazement as the normally short-tempered Pomeranian immediately responded to her command. He zoomed out of the yard and past the deck.

Loretta walked back inside the house. She looked through the front windows and watched as Pauline attached Nigel's leash to his collar. Milo raced to the window and uttered a low, guttural growl. He swiped at the windowpane with his large paws. Pauline looked up and scowled at the house. She yanked Nigel's leash and scurried quickly down the road.

"I can't tell a thing about that woman," Loretta told the angry cat. "One minute she's fluttering around acting like a mad, crazy person, and the next she is almost human."

Milo offered no wisdom and trotted off toward his litter box. Loretta returned to her bedroom and took a fast shower. She had no idea what the day might bring but decided the best way to start it was to enjoy her first cup of coffee outside by the lake. She intended to make the practice a habit. Despite the events that had happened so far, it was time to enjoy her surroundings and remind herself that the decision to move to Florida was not a mistake.

Thirty minutes later, Loretta gazed over the lake with a mug of hot coffee in her hand. Her brother's words came back to her. He'd told her there was nothing about Breezy Lake that made him happy to be there. Loretta reviewed the first three days in her new home. She had met a strangely dressed busybody with an obnoxious, yipping dog who doubled as a real human being at the weirdest times. She had appeared in front of the Clubhouse Cooks committee and was told she could participate in cooking dinner for the entire village. Then later, one of the committee members wound up dead in the middle of the club-house, where the dinner was supposed to take place. Following that, there was the meeting with the deputy sheriff, who seemed suspicious of her simply because she was a newcomer and had discovered the body.

Funny thing was, she hadn't seen or heard another word from the deputy since her unfortunate fainting spell. It was just as well. She'd been almost certain the officer posted outside of her room at the hospital was there because she was a serious suspect in Nina's death.

Loretta drained her coffee and admired the lake a

while longer. She shivered when she considered the temperature she had seen on her phone's weather app when she first woke up that morning. The app still listed the weather back in the New Hampshire area. Her former neighbors and customers at the bistro were greeted with a frigid twenty-degree morning, while she was sitting behind her new home dressed in a lightweight cardigan enjoying the breeze off the lake. The morning temperature hovered in the low seventies.

Clarence was wrong. There was plenty to be happy about at her new home. She watched the early sunlight dancing over the ripples in the lake. Something stirred in her soul when she gave the water her full attention. The water moved to its own rhythm. The houses on the other side of the lake appeared quaint and charming against the tranquil water. Tall trees lined the bank and stood over the houses like proud sentries.

Flies moved in clouds over the surface of the lake. Once in a while, a fish broke the surface of the water and flopped its body high in the air. Loretta smiled with each launch out of the water. The action took nothing away from the tranquility. The homes surrounding her might not be worth what she could find in more expensive retirement neighborhoods in Florida, but Loretta was quite sure she had a million-dollar view.

CHAPTER EIGHT

Loretta returned to her house a short time after she finished her second cup of coffee. Stacks of boxes lined the far wall of the living room. She had made fast work of unpacking the kitchen the first night she was there. Her beloved kitchen was the first thing she wanted access to, outside of her clothing and personal items.

She walked past the boxes once again. Compared to her home in Herring Heights, there was nothing remarkable about the four walls. Inside, her house was plain and beige. The features of her new home were simple and functional. There was no granite in the kitchen or marble in the bathroom. The floors beneath her were aesthetically pleasing, but something she could easily pick up at a big box hardware store.

It wasn't that her previous home was a mansion or anything, but it was in a nice neighborhood inside a gated community. She had worked for years to afford an upper middle-class life, and she assumed her former husband had done the same. As it turned out, he had been working for himself and his other interests while she had done her best for the two of them.

Bitterness suited no one, Loretta told herself. As much as the trajectory of her life had been affected by it, the past was the past. She had no desire to allow it to stain the pristine view she had of the lake through her kitchen window.

Instead, Loretta decided a nice morning walk was in order. Her physician back home had educated her on the benefits of regular exercise, and time spent out in the sunshine was even better than a stroll around an inside track or on a treadmill. Loretta slipped her feet into her favorite shoes and headed out the front door. She clipped her house key onto the small ring attached to her phone case and headed to her left, opposite of the way to the front entrance. Exploring the neighborhood sounded like a good idea.

The sun was a little higher in the sky than it was while she sat outside with her coffee, but the air was still pleasant. According to the map she had been given with her house contract and neighborhood information, a small set of shops and businesses had been planned around the lake, essentially dividing the houses into quarters, and providing a select number of services to the residents. Loretta's home itself was situated halfway between two of those sections. As she walked, she passed a small vegetable market and a dry cleaning service. One or two small buildings advertised bait and boating supplies. There were two coffee shops on opposite sides of the lake, both of which she couldn't wait to check out.

Loretta heard the familiar yipping of her least favorite dog as she passed the dry cleaners. She looked up to see Pauline and Brigitte bounding toward her. A third woman walked along with them, though the smile on her face made her appear much more approachable in comparison.

"Loretta," Pauline called out. Her voice carried far, possibly to the other side of the lake. "Loretta, we have some news."

"Did they find the killer?" Loretta asked immediately. She was hopeful the murderer would be quickly discovered and apprehended. As much as she loved Milo, he was not very useful as a nightly alarm system. Perhaps she should look into a noisy little dog like Nigel, but a quick glance at his snarling little face relieved her of that notion.

"No, no," Pauline said. She swiped at the air and pulled Nigel back from the third woman's ankles. She leaned forward and looked around before lowering her voice and leaning in. "The Carpenter family is here. They are going through Nina's house and her belongings."

"Her husband died years ago, but his sister is here to get whatever she wants from Nina's things," Brigitte added.

The third woman smiled tolerantly. "The family of the deceased is here to collect her things and prepare for her memorial service on Sea Glass Island," she said. "What we would like to do here is provide meals for the family while they are in town."

"I'm sorry," Loretta said. "We have not been properly introduced. I'm Loretta Barksdale, neighborhood newbie."

"Kelly Crenshaw," the woman said. "Community Coordinator here at Breezy Lake Village."

"Oh, that's great. It's a pleasure to meet you." She instantly liked the woman.

Loretta felt a burst of warmth in her middle. "I would love to help out with some meals. I was preparing a great deal of rolls for the community dinner tonight."

"That got canceled," Brigitte interrupted.

"I figured as much," Loretta said.

"I understand that you were the unfortunate soul who first found the body," Kelly said. "That must have been traumatic."

"It wasn't pleasant," Loretta said. "Thankfully, Pauline and Nigel were right outside."

Pauline beamed. "I'm the one who called the cops."

"That she was," Loretta said. She kept her comments about the rest of their interaction to herself.

"If you need someone to talk to, I am a pretty good listener," Kelly continued.

"I have no doubt about that," Loretta said. "Anyway, please tell me how I can help. I used to run a bistro back home."

Kelly smiled. "If you have a covered dish you could bring over at about six o'clock tonight, that would be wonderful," she said. "I think we need more main dishes, but feel free to bring along any of those rolls, too."

"Yes," Pauline said. "We are short on main dishes. We have plenty of sides."

"Desserts, too," Brigitte added. "I'm bringing two pans of dump cake."

"That's wonderful, Brigitte," Kelly said. Loretta wondered if her patience with the two women was an acquired skill.

"Do you know how many we're feeding?" Loretta asked.

"At least three dozen," Pauline said.

"There are that many family members?" Loretta asked. She was surprised by the number.

"Nina had three children of her own, and her husband had five or six," Kelly said. "Pauline is correct."

Loretta smiled. She had just the dish in mind. "I'll drop off something around six, then," she said. "I suppose her house will be easy to find."

"It's three houses up from the clubhouse," Brigitte added quickly.

"You should have no problem finding it," Kelly said. She smiled pleasantly and extended her hand to Loretta once again. Loretta found herself wondering how old Kelly was and how she came to serve the people of the small retirement village. She was closer to Loretta's age than many of the other people around. Her face was relatively unlined, though it bore the maturity of one who had lived through their forties and possibly fifties. She was a pretty woman but not to distraction. Her auburn hair was cut just above her shoulders. If she wore makeup, it was limited to simple mascara and translucent lip gloss.

"We'll be there around that time as well with our own dishes." Pauline cast a sideways glance at Kelly, who appeared undeterred by her tone of voice.

"Good, then. I'll see you all a bit later." Loretta turned to head back, dodging Nigel just in time before he had a chance to chase her down.

CHAPTER NINE

After a brisk walk around the lake, Loretta planned to stop by the market on her way home. Her freezer contained several free-range chickens from a farm she'd passed by on her first day in town, but her pantry and vegetable crispers were empty.

Loretta felt good as she turned off the road and headed into the small, metal building that served as the vegetable market. Large windows covered the front of the building. She walked through the displays of fresh vegetables set under the covered area in the front of the market.

"Morning," an older man said from a wooden stand next to the door.

"Good morning," Loretta said.

"You new around here?" the man asked.

Loretta nodded. "I sure am," she said. "Loretta Barksdale is my name. I moved in about a dozen houses back up that way." She pointed in the direction of her home.

"You're the one who found Nina Carpenter's body, aren't you?" The man's friendly smile fell.

Loretta released the small yellow onion she had grabbed from the display in front of her. "Unfortunately, yes, I am," she said. She sighed and turned to leave.

"Heck of a way to start out in a new place," the man said. "Sorry you had to go through that."

Loretta looked up at him. "Thank you. I feel bad for Nina's family," she said.

"Oh, of course." He slipped off his stool and reached for a large canvas bag. "Here you are. On the house. Use it each time you stop by."

"Thank you," Loretta said. "I don't think I know your name."

"Edwin," he said. "Edwin Jackson."

The deep lines in his russet skin revealed his advanced age, but the glint in his eyes belied it. His whole face grinned when he smiled. "It's very nice to meet you, Mr. Jackson."

"Oh, you'd better call me Edwin," he said. "Otherwise, some of these old gossips around are going to get the wrong idea about you and me. Are you sure you're old enough to be living here? You don't look a day over forty."

"Well, you're sweet, but I am fifty and a couple months old. I qualify to live here, I promise."

"I sure hope you find what you need. Let me know if you need any help," Edwin said.

"Well, I'm going to make a chicken pot pie to take over to the Carpenter family," Loretta said. "I need three pounds of onions, five pounds of potatoes, celery, carrots, and fresh thyme. Do you carry fresh herbs?"

"Sure do," Edwin said. "Grow them myself on my property. You can pick out whatever you like while I get the rest of your things. Hand me that bag back, and I'll fill it up for you."

Loretta handed over the canvas shopping bag and then walked around until she found the fresh herbs on the back wall. She was pleased to find a small cooler with fresh milk, half and half, and heavy cream. She selected a quart of cream and a pound of butter. "This little market of yours has just about everything I need."

He set the filled bag down and picked up another one from behind the counter. "Well, that's good to know. Why don't you look over what I picked out for you while I ring everything up?"

Edwin gave her the total, and Loretta handed over the bank card she kept in the back of her phone case.

"Here you go, young lady." He handed over the two bags. "You let me know if you need anything else. I can bring in meat or coffee or anything you might need for your pantry. I just need to know what you want and how often you want it."

"Well, that is incredible," Loretta said. "Any chance you can get whole coffee beans?"

"As long as you don't tell anybody else, I'll get them in for you," Edwin said with a wink. "You just bring along a list with you the next time you come by, and I'll have anything you want within a day or two."

"You got it," Loretta said.

"Of course, I would be glad to receive any leftovers from those meals you put together with the Clubhouse Cooks," he said. Loretta told him she would see what she could do and left with her groceries in her arms.

When she arrived at home, she hefted her groceries inside and set them on the kitchen counter. After she put everything away, Loretta decided that she would rest for a while and read her newest novel before diving into her chicken pot pie.

Two hours later, she stood in front of her freezer, deciding which of her frozen chickens she would take out. She selected the largest one and set it in the sink. She ran water over the bird until she could easily remove the outer wrapping. She removed the plastic and rinsed the chicken before placing it in the pressure cooker, then made her selections on the electronic keypad and secured the lid.

While the chicken cooked, Loretta searched her cabinets for her favorite deep-dish pie plate. She set it on the counter and quickly washed it with hot water. Even if she had wrapped it carefully in packing paper, she wanted to make sure it was squeaky clean before she started using it. While the pie plate dried, Loretta pulled her flour canister from the cupboard and found her other ingredients. She mixed a pinch of salt in her measured flour then cut in shortening for her pie crust. She delicately rolled out the crust in two sections and then set them aside.

A little while later, she pulled a large skillet out of the cabinet and plopped a dollop of butter in the center of it. While the pan heated up, Loretta placed her vegetables on her large cutting board. She diced two onions, sliced up the carrots and celery, and then chopped the fresh thyme and set it aside in a small bowl.

Loretta slowly added the onions to the pan, then the celery and carrots. She stirred the vegetables until the onions were nearly translucent. She removed the pan from the heat for a moment, then turned down the burner. While the vegetables sat, Loretta quickly removed the chicken from the pressure cooker and placed it on a cutting board to cool. She placed the skillet on the burner again and turned to the fridge for the cream and more butter. While the butter melted, she quickly sliced the chicken, and set it aside to retrieve the flour canister again.

The skillet sizzled with the butter, and Loretta added the chicken and a dash of flour over the top. She added the cut thyme and sprinkled salt, pepper, and turmeric over it. She stirred the mixture to distribute the seasonings and then began to slowly add the heavy cream. She continued to stir the mixture, taste testing at one or two minute intervals to ensure the homemade taste she loved.

After the mixture was thoroughly cooked and adequately thickened, Loretta set the skillet aside once again and carefully covered the deep-dish pie plate with the bottom crust. She pricked the bottom with a fork, then slowly poured the hot filling over it. She finished by carefully laying the top crust over the filling. She pulled a sharp, thin filet knife from the knife block and slowly dotted the design of an acorn and two leaves in the top. She trimmed the crust and fluted the edges, then placed the dish in a hot oven and turned on the oven timer, eager for the finished product.

CHAPTER TEN

Loretta had quickly tidied up the kitchen and moved to the back deck while the pot pie baked. The savory aromas that wafted through the screen door tempted her as she rested. She chided herself for failing to reserve a small portion of the dough and the filling for herself for dinner.

As soon as the oven timer chimed, Loretta stood and moved swiftly inside to the kitchen. She turned the oven off and set the deep pie plate on a cooling rack. She smiled at the outcome. The crust had browned to a deep golden color, and the leaf and acorn pattern she had cut in the middle of the top crust added a homey appearance to the dish. It was exactly how she had hoped it would turn out.

When the dish was cooled sufficiently, Loretta slipped her shoes back on her feet. She checked her appearance in the bathroom mirror, then pulled a new sweater from her closet. As soon as she was ready, Loretta placed the lid carefully over the pie plate and set it in the travel carrier she had purchased to go along with it. She had considered driving her car around the lake to the Carpenter house but decided to take advantage of the evening air and ride the three-wheel bicycle she had bought for herself before her move. The bike was used and a few years old, but she reasoned the purchase made sense for her new life-style in retirement.

She carefully placed the pot pie in the metal basket behind her seat. She backed the bicycle out of the small lean-to next to her garage and pointed the wheel toward the road. Her arms and legs felt good and strong as she made her way slowly around the lake toward the clubhouse. She caught glimpses of the lake through the houses. As she passed, she noticed several gardens, mostly flower gardens. One home was surrounded by multiple vegetable gardens. Nearly every available inch of ground had been planted, and Loretta wondered if the home belonged to her new friend Edwin.

Fifteen minutes after she left her house, Loretta slowed down and veered off the road toward the small house a few doors down from the clubhouse. She parked her bike across the street. Parked cars filled the driveway and street in front of the house, leaving her little choice. Like all the homes surrounding the lake, Nina's was a decades-old modular home just like her own, but the addition of newer siding and landscaping gave it a quaint, New England feel. Loretta approached the front door and knocked with her free hand while she balanced the pot pie in the other.

The door opened a few seconds later. A man around her own age stood there. "More food?"

"This is for the family, yes." Loretta walked past the man and stepped into the open living room area. At least thirty people milled around the space. She nodded to several strangers on her way into the kitchen. She spotted Brigitte standing in front of the back door in the dining room area. Brigitte's face was the only one she recognized at the moment. She met Loretta's eyes and jerked her head toward a long table. Loretta walked through the kitchen and set the dish on the table next to the others.

"Loretta?" She turned around and spotted Wally

Neville coming toward her. His eyes appeared red and puffy. He held his hands out as he approached. "Thank you so much for stopping by with your dish. We certainly have enough food to keep the family well fed."

"Well, I'm grateful I can help," Loretta said. "After all, this is my community now. I'm more than happy to help out where I can."

Wally stared into her eyes for an uncomfortable amount of time. "Nina was right about you," he whispered. Tears brimmed his eyes. "She said you were a good addition to our community, and she was never wrong about people." He turned suddenly and rushed off down the hall. Loretta watched him leave, a little stunned at both his emotional reaction and the abruptness of his departure from their conversation.

"What did you make?" Brigitte asked from behind her. Loretta turned back around.

"Chicken pot pie. I made it all from scratch."

"Is there another option than from scratch?" Brigitte whispered with a grin. Loretta looked past her at the table. The pie plate had been removed from the carrier.

"Did you see it?" Loretta asked, hoping her presentation was well received.

"I spied on what you made," Brigitte said. "I haven't had a chance to see you in action, so to speak. I wanted to know if your cooking would live up to your boasting."

"Boasting? I never boasted," Loretta replied. She forced herself to keep her voice low.

"Either way, that pot pie smells divine," Brigitte said. "Have you seen Pauline? I thought she would be here by now." Her voice trailed off as she wandered away from Loretta.

"Excuse me." The man from the front door approached her in the middle of the kitchen. "We have a small table set up in the backyard to honor my mother. We have some refreshments and drinks for community members and a guest book. Would you mind signing the book? There is a paper there for you to write down the dish you left as well. I noticed it wasn't in a disposable pan."

Loretta felt her face redden. "I just moved in," she explained. "I haven't had a chance to stock my kitchen with disposable pans."

He leaned in a little closer. "Listen, my mom lived here for a long time. Do yourself a favor and stock up," he said. "You have no idea how often you will be called upon to bring dishes over for families."

"Good tip," Loretta said. "Nina was your mom?"

He nodded. "I'm Tate, her oldest," he said. "My mom was a big member of this community. She was pretty well loved, as you can see."

"I liked her from the start," Loretta offered. "She seemed very nice and…"

"Fair?" Tate finished. "A lot of people loved my mom for her ability to remain neutral in conflicts. She was a professional mediator before she retired."

"Fair is a good word," Loretta said. "I'm sorry for your loss."

"Thank you." He excused himself to meet with another person. Loretta walked past several small groups of people and headed out the back door. She wanted to sign the guest book as requested, then make her way back home. Her introverted self was beginning to react to the sheer number of people packed into such a small space.

When Loretta opened the back door, the fresh air hit her like a life preserver. She inhaled deeply and stepped onto the patio. Much like the front of the house, Nina's backyard was a carefully landscaped garden. Loretta counted four separate seating areas under the wooden pergola that covered the deck. She spotted the small table with the guest book and pen. A folding table filled with bottled water and other drinks had been set up in the grass next to the patio. She bypassed the drink table and picked up the pen to write down her name and a description of her pie plate.

"It's a beautiful evening," Kelly said from behind her. Loretta turned around and instantly smiled.

"Yes, it is," Loretta said. "Looks like a fairly good turnout, too."

Loretta noted Kelly's wardrobe had changed. She was dressed in a simple blue pantsuit. "You will soon find out that these informal memorial services happen about once every other month, though not usually under these circumstances," she said, peering over Loretta's shoulder at the guest book. "It's a good idea to invest in a stock of aluminum pans."

"So I hear."

"Oh, if you will excuse me, I see Nina's youngest daughter and her husband," Kelly said. "I have yet to speak with them."

"Of course," Loretta replied. She turned around and surveyed the crowd. Despite the refreshing breeze, there were still quite a few too many people gathered around for her liking. Going back through the house was the last thing she wanted to do. Loretta inhaled and walked out toward the lake. She considered walking down to the small boat dock for a moment, but decided she needed to get back on her bike and pedal home.

She smiled at a few faces as she made her way toward a large trellis covered in a thorny rose bush at the corner of the house. As soon as she approached, she could hear muffled sobs. Loretta took another step, prepared to offer some comfort to what she presumed to be another of Nina's children. Instead, she found Wally sobbing against the wall, concealed by the trellis. Loretta decided disturbing him was not her place. She turned back to the house and wound her way through more small collections of people and around the attached garage.

To her surprise, a small door leading into the garage was open. Loretta instantly thought the door was a better design choice than she had seen at her own house, but her thoughts were interrupted. Two men she could not see were inside the garage. She heard their conversation and paused to listen. It was an incredibly rude thing to do, that she knew, but their severe whispers told her the conversation was tense. Her curiosity got the better of her.

"I told you," one of the men said. "That money just disappeared!"

"Money doesn't just disappear, Reg," the other man said. Loretta's mind raced. Reg was familiar. She had heard someone refer to a Reginald at the meeting of the Clubhouse Cooks committee.

"I know that, but it isn't just the Clubhouse Cooks. It's the entire village. Money has gone missing here and there. It's happening all over the place."

"Last week, we held a fundraising drive for the golf club," the other man said. "Over twelve hundred dollars was raised at the bake sale. Do you know what we wound up with at the end of the day? Nine hundred and fifty bucks."

"That's all that was reported?" Reginald asked.

"No," the other voice hissed. "That's all that was returned! I was there, man. I saw the cash and even counted it myself."

"Okay, but how sure are you that the original number was over twelve hundred, Clay?" Clay. Loretta memorized the name.

"I never left that table during the fundraiser, except to relieve myself as needed," Clay said. "I kept a running tally in my head as the day went on. I know we were over twelve hundred, but I can't tell you the exact amount down to the cent."

"I believe every word you're saying," Reginald said. "It's just that you and I both know what this means, and we have to be very careful before we go pointing fingers."

"Do you make it a habit to eavesdrop on people often?" Loretta turned around quickly. She found Gwen Neville standing behind her.

"Oh, no," Loretta stammered. "I was just, you know."

Gwen's face split into a smile. "I know you overheard them and waited in case something was wrong and they needed help," she said with a smile. "I'm the same way, but let me give you a word of warning. In this community, the men are worse than the women with their gossip and invented crises. It's almost like they need mysteries to solve and problems to fix."

Loretta smiled, though she was a little unsure about Gwen's explanation. "That's good to know," she said. "I think I'm just on edge."

"That sounds like a perfectly reasonable response," Gwen said. "Now tell me, are you up for a coffee date Thursday morning? I have a busy schedule tomorrow but would love to meet you the next day."

"Sure." Loretta smiled. "Just tell me where and when."

Gwen nodded. "How about eight at Mama Bee's?"

"Mama Bee's?" Loretta asked.

"Yeah, it is on the north side of the lake," Gwen said. She pointed in the general direction.

"I will see you Thursday at eight, then," Loretta said. She left Gwen with a smile and headed for the road.

CHAPTER ELEVEN

Loretta was glad to see her three-wheeled beach cruiser bike was still where she left it parked. After the murder of one of the residents, she was unsure whether theft was also a legitimate problem in the village. She turned back in the direction of her own home and pedaled along.

She drove past the clubhouse and slowed down. She spotted a white car with a "Sunshine County Sheriff" decal on the side of the door. She looked around for evidence of a uniformed deputy. Deputy Hargraves saw her and waved her over to the car.

"I guess I know what the name of the county is now," Loretta mumbled to herself as she biked over. She angled the bike as she slowed down and parked behind the cruiser, away from the middle of the road.

"What's going on, Deputy?" She swung her legs over to the side as he approached her.

"Where's your helmet, Ms. Barksdale?" he asked her.

"You called me over to chastise me for not wearing a helmet?" Loretta asked.

"No, I actually called you over to see how you were doing after your little fainting spell." Deputy Hargraves smiled. "Although it is advisable for you to have a helmet."

Loretta cleared her throat. She looked down at her hands and nodded her head. "I agree with you that a helmet is a good idea. Unfortunately, I have no idea where mine is," she said. "And to answer your question, I am much better. Thank you."

"That's good to hear. I truly didn't mean to cause any harm when I was speaking to you about the death of Nina Carpenter," he said. Loretta read sincerity in his eyes.

"I believe you were doing your job, Deputy," she said softly. "Tell me, how is the investigation going?"

Deputy Hargraves exhaled quickly and pushed his hat back. "I have nothing," he said. "Aside from more questions for several people, including you."

"So, I'm still a suspect?" Loretta asked.

"Not a suspect, but everyone is a person of

interest at this point in time. You said that you had just met Nina at a committee meeting on the day that she died. Is that correct?"

Loretta nodded. "It's sort of a prerequisite to living here that you have to belong to one club or another," she offered. "For me, cooking is basically my thing. I owned and ran a bistro back home."

"When you were at this meeting, did you witness any interactions between Nina and the others? I've heard various points of view, but you have a unique perspective as an outsider."

"Ouch."

"You know what I mean," he said.

"Well." Loretta thought for a moment. "I saw Nina react to some mild bullying by a couple of busy-bodies. She was fair. That's the same word her son used to describe her."

"Who were the busybodies?" Deputy Hargraves asked.

"Pauline Pendleton and Brigitte Waldorf," Loretta said. "They're both very busy keeping track of everything. Pauline told me she is the unofficial mayor of the village."

"What did Brigitte say to her?" the deputy asked.

"During the committee meeting, Brigitte had a few pointed questions for me and why I sold my business. Nina stepped in and reminded her that I was under no obligation to answer her questions," Loretta said.

"Is that all you witnessed?"

Loretta shook her head. "Later on, Pauline and Brigitte cornered me and read a laundry list of things I needed to do for the upcoming dinner, which was subsequently canceled, of course. Nina stopped them from ordering me to prepare enough food for a small army. She asked me to simply prepare a few dozen dinner rolls or whatever I could handle in the given time."

"What was Brigitte's reaction to that?"

"She did what Nina told her," Loretta recalled. "Apparently, there was a packet of information Brigitte was responsible for getting to me, and she failed to do that until Nina called her out for it. Brigitte did as she requested, but there really was no reaction."

Deputy Hargraves nodded his head. He gazed toward the lake. "I see. Have you noticed anything else? I would love to hear your thoughts. I'll admit that I have nothing much to go on, and everything helps in a situation like this one."

Loretta shrugged. "I've heard a few things here

and there, but I don't know enough to tell you whether or not what I heard is suspicious."

"Why don't you just share with me what you know and let me figure that part out?" he said.

"Okay, well, just a bit ago, I heard two men in the garage at Nina's house discussing money missing from a fundraiser," Loretta said.

"Who were these two men?" he asked.

Loretta sighed. "I feel horrible about this, but one was named Reginald and the other one was named Clay," she said.

"So, you think they were the ones taking the money?"

Loretta shook her head. "No, not at all. It was more like they were trying to figure out how it was happening and who might be behind it all."

"Okay," the deputy said. "Anything else?"

Loretta shook her head slowly. "No, I was discovered, you might say."

"By whom?"

"Gwen Neville," Loretta said. "She asked me if I often eavesdrop on other people."

"That's awkward," Deputy Hargraves said. "Are you friends with Gwen?"

"I might be," Loretta said. "We're supposed to have coffee in a couple of days."

"Enjoy your coffee, but please don't discuss anything we have spoken about here," he said. "I've been very careful about the information that has been discussed, and I would like to keep it that way. People sure do have a lot to say around here, and rumors spread fast."

"I have a question for you, Deputy," Loretta said. She mounted the bike again. "Is this a safe place to live? Did I make a mistake investing every last penny I had in a home here?"

"Until now, I would have told you that this is the safest area in the whole state, but after what happened, I'm not so sure what's going on."

CHAPTER TWELVE

Loretta was halfway home when she realized she'd forgotten to tell the deputy about finding Wally in tears. The detective's questions swirled in her head. She had never been one for suspense novels. Historical books were more her speed, but she wondered if there was something she was missing.

Clearly, Deputy Hargraves had his eye on Brigitte. Was Pauline's clumsy sidekick capable of killing someone? She had no idea what the backstory might be between Brigitte and the dead woman, but she had an inkling Brigitte was harmless.

There had to be more going on behind the scenes. Loretta heard with her own ears that a money scandal existed in the community. The men in the garage mentioned twelve hundred dollars raised at a fundraiser for the golf club, but several hundred dollars less were actually turned in following the bake sale. If every member of the Breezy Lake community was asked to belong to one club or another, Loretta figured the actual amount of misappropriated funds could be much higher.

Loretta heard a familiar bark. Nigel, the Pomeranian, strained on his leash as she rounded the curve to her home. She was surprised to see not only Pauline but Brigitte standing on the road in front of her driveway. Their heads were bent together in deep conversation.

"What are you doing, Loretta?" Pauline asked when she spotted her.

Loretta veered past them into her driveway and hit her brakes. "I live here."

"I don't think you should be riding a bike." Brigitte folded her arms over her chest and glared at her.

"I really don't know why you think that, but I am wondering what you two are doing here. It's getting late and I'm tired, so if you don't mind, I'm going inside."

"Why are you tired?" Pauline asked.

"Probably from running around here doing things we don't know about." Brigitte smirked.

"Be quiet," Pauline sneered. She turned back to Loretta. Her eyes softened with concern.

"I just rode this bike for the first time, and it turns out it's quite the workout. Plus, that chicken pot pie I made for Nina's family took two full hours."

"Well, you left Nina's house without saying a word," Pauline said. Her face tightened back into her default look.

Loretta sighed. "I never saw you," she said. "I spoke briefly with Brigitte."

Pauline turned to Brigitte. "Why didn't you make her wait for me?"

"I'm not usually persuaded by someone making me do anything," Loretta said.

"Anyway, did you see Wally and Gwen?" Pauline asked.

"Wally and Gwen?" Loretta asked.

Brigitte stepped forward. Her face beamed as she spoke. "Yes, their marriage is something else," she said. "Somebody said Wally was crying over Nina's death."

"Maybe they were friends," Loretta offered.

"Or maybe they were involved in an illicit affair," Brigitte said, almost bouncing in anticipation.

"An illicit affair? In a retirement village?" Loretta asked.

"What? You don't think seniors are capable of having affairs?" Pauline asked.

"Don't ever assume anything about the people around here," Brigitte said. "You have no idea how many things are going on behind closed doors."

"Well, maybe I don't, but as someone who has been through a divorce, I don't like the idea of gossiping about someone else's marriage."

"Who's gossiping?" Pauline countered. "Is that what you think we're doing?"

"Well, what are you doing?" Loretta asked.

"Discussing," Brigitte said. "That's what we're doing. Haven't you ever had a discussion with a friend before?"

Loretta shook her head rather than answer the question. "I'm meeting Gwen on Thursday for coffee," she said, hoping the news would tone down the conversation.

"Well, you should watch out what you say to her," Pauline said.

"What do you mean?" Loretta asked. "What should I be careful about saying?"

"Anything about her husband," Pauline said. "She is very jealous about Wally. I've seen her fly into a rage over nothing."

"Alright. I hadn't planned to say anything to her

about her husband, but I will be cautious. Anything else?"

"Don't try to talk to her about anything to do with money," Brigitte said. "It seems like Gwen is in charge of everything financial around here, and she does not appreciate anyone questioning her on how she keeps things going."

"Brigitte is right about that," Pauline said. "Gwen is very particular about the community treasury. She does not like anyone asking her questions about it. She said it is inappropriate to ask those types of questions in public."

"Well, maybe she's right," Loretta said. "But the good news is, I don't really care about that."

Brigitte's eyes widened. She turned to Pauline and pounded her hand on her arm. "Do you remember when that whole thing blew up about the founder's fee?"

"Will you please stop hitting me?" Pauline scolded her. "And yes, I remember."

Brigitte ignored Pauline's comment and turned to Loretta. "There used to be this charge added to every house purchase whenever anyone moved into the community," she said. "A couple of people got really upset about it and took it to a lawyer in Tallahassee."

"What happened?" Loretta asked. She was mildly

interested in hearing more, mainly because she had just bought into the community herself.

"They took the case to court," Pauline said. She bent down to pick Nigel up. "A judge ruled that the additional charge was illegal."

"Gwen lost her mind. She said that the whole point of it was to help support clubs and organizations within the village," Brigitte said. "That's when the fundraising went crazy. She told everyone that the housing market here would suffer if there weren't as many recreational activities and clubs."

"Because people usually come to places like these to be a part of the community," Pauline said. "We've always done some fundraising. At least since I moved here."

Brigitte turned to her. "That's a really, really long time," she said.

"Shut up, Brigitte," Pauline said. She put Nigel back on the ground and waved at Loretta. "Have fun having coffee with your new friend. See you around." Her hair flounced as she walked off.

"I think you know what you did," Brigitte said as a parting comment. Loretta waited until she hurried to catch up with Pauline and rolled her eyes. Apparently, she dared to have a friend outside of the pair of them. She had a hard time keeping track of whether Pauline considered her an interloper or a friend. She pushed her bike back under the lean-to and opened the garage door. She walked inside and took a seat at her kitchen table. After a moment, she rose to pour herself a glass of ice water. Loretta set the water on the table and stared out the picture window at the lake for a moment. Brigitte's words bounced around in her head. She wondered about the community's finances. She also wondered about her own.

Loretta considered retrieving her own paperwork from the stack of files in one of her spare rooms, but her body was tired. The feeling chased the other thoughts from her head. Instead of looking over her contract, she grabbed her book and headed to the large, comfortable chair in her living room.

CHAPTER THIRTEEN

Loretta woke early the next morning to the sound of a loud motor in her right ear. She turned her head just far enough to feel the mound of fur hit her face. "Milo, do you want something?" she asked, her voice muffled when he sat down on the lower half of her head. Instead of moving or having the decency to explain himself, the large cat continued to nuzzle her face.

"You smell like fish," Loretta declared. She rolled the cat over in her bed and sat up. The clock on her end table read five minutes after six in the morning. Apparently, it took some time to shake off old habits like waking up at the crack of dawn. She threw back the covers and padded to the ensuite bathroom, then headed straight to the kitchen to start a pot of coffee.

Milo followed and stationed himself in front of the glass doors that led to the back deck. He seemed mesmerized by something outdoors. The sun had yet to rise, so Loretta was unsure just what he was watching. The moment the large feline hunkered down in an attack stance and began his low, guttural growl, Loretta had a feeling her least favorite canine had returned to her yard.

"Nigel," she muttered under her breath when she stood up and spotted the dog through the window above the sink. Rather than throw the sliding door open, Loretta decided to take it to the source. She walked through her house to the front door and opened it to see Pauline waiting for Nigel in the road in front of her house.

"Pauline," Loretta said when she opened the front door. "Your dog is ruining my yard."

"I'm not trespassing," Pauline said defensively.

"But your dog, Pauline," Loretta said. "Please stop letting him off the leash at my house. I don't want to spend my days in the hospital with a broken ankle because I fell into one of his traps."

"How large can the holes be from those tiny paws of his?" She rolled her eyes and bent down to reattach the leash to Nigel's collar when he came bounding back from the backyard to her side. Loretta said nothing as the pair walked away.

Around seven, Loretta set her coffee mug in the sink and headed to her bedroom. She intended to gather clothing for a quick shower but found herself dressing in workout clothes and heading out the door for a morning walk. This time, she was determined to make her way around the entire lake before making her way back home.

As it turned out, Loretta was not the only Breezy Lake resident out for an early-morning walk. She waved at several people, most of them faces she did not yet recognize. About a quarter of the way around the lake, Loretta spotted Kelly dressed in blue yoga pants and a matching windbreaker.

"Good morning." Kelly paused her walk and smiled.

"Good morning," Loretta said. She sipped from her metal water bottle.

"I need one of those," Kelly said, indicating the water bottle.

"Oh, I have a ton of these at home," Loretta said. "I hate to admit how many of them I brought with me."

Kelly nodded. "I'll have to look for one the next

time I leave the village," she said. "I don't get out much anymore."

"So, you do live here?" Loretta asked.

"I live in my mother's house. Like you, I've just reached the age requirement, but I'd been staying here to care for her, and the Village Council didn't give us a hard time about it. When I landed the job as Community Coordinator, I decided to stick around for good after she passed."

"I'm sorry for your loss, but happy to have you here," Loretta said. "What is the Village Council?"

"Oh, it's just like it sounds. While there is no official municipality here in terms of the state of Florida, the council serves just like a board of aldermen or a city council. Only in our case, there is no mayor."

"So, the village just goes with a majority vote?" Loretta asked.

Kelly nodded. "You seem fairly knowledgeable about small town politics," she said. "Have you had any experience with it before? If you have, you better prepare to be asked to do more than just the Clubhouse Cooks as soon as word gets out."

Loretta shook her head. "My only experience is in the town where my bistro was located. I had to go before several committees before I could open the doors for the first time. Believe me, I have zero interest in politics," she said.

"Well, then," Kelly said. She began walking in place. "I won't bother you about it again." She smiled and gave a little wave before heading off again for her walk in the opposite direction.

"Good morning," Loretta said to several passersby as she continued walking. She was grateful that she had not run into Brigitte and Pauline. Perhaps she had gone late enough in the morning to miss any sign of the pair.

"Good morning," Loretta said again to an unfamiliar man as he passed her. He appeared to be in his upper sixties, which made him one of the younger men she had seen.

"Morning. Is it Lois?" he asked her.

She slowed her walk again. "Loretta," she said with a smile. "And you are?"

"Clay," the man said. "Clay Fulton. I'm a member of the Village Council."

"Okay," Loretta said. "Kelly was just telling me about the council."

"Are you interested in serving?" Clay asked. His eyes widened.

"No, no," Loretta said, shaking her head quickly.

"My background is culinary. I have no interest in the government in any form."

Clay nodded his head. "You sound like most newcomers around here, but that's okay," he said. "We need people in other places. Have you chosen a club yet?"

"The Clubhouse Cooks," Loretta said. "I've already appeared before the committee, and I was the unfortunate person who came upon Nina Carpenter's body."

Clay's face immediately fell. "That is such a tragic thing," he said. "I should get going."

"Wait, before you go," Loretta said. "I have to admit something. I overheard a conversation between you and another man yesterday in the garage at Nina's home. I was there to drop something off."

"You were eavesdropping?" he asked her. His eyes narrowed.

Loretta shook her head quickly. "Not intention-ally, but I did hear a little about money concerns."

Clay nodded. "I can see why that would upset someone who is new around here," he said. "We have been trying to figure out where the money is going for months at this point, but let me give you a little piece of advice. Stay out of it. Unless you're going to get involved with the government as you put it, keep your nose out of those matters. Gwen has the financial well-being of the village handled. Trust me on that. Good day, Loretta." He swiftly resumed his walk, leaving her standing alone with her thoughts in the middle of the road.

CHAPTER FOURTEEN

"I'm not here to start anything," Pauline called out to her two hours later. She stood out in front of Loretta's house again.

"You know, you're welcome to come to my door and knock or send a text if you have something to say to me," Loretta said. She stood in the middle of the garage. The overhead door was open. Pauline stood in the road in front of the driveway.

"Well, I don't have your cell phone number, so I can't text you and I know how you feel about people trespassing on your property," Pauline said.

Loretta hung her head for a second and sighed. "I'll give you my number," she said. "I just don't like it when you let Nigel off of his leash and he digs up my yard."

"I'm here to invite you to an informal get-together at the clubhouse this afternoon," Pauline said, still pouting. "We were just wondering if you could bring some homemade bread. Loaves are fine. Of course, rolls would be better, but no one wants to put you out."

Loretta bit the inside of her lip. She wanted to laugh out loud given the long list of dishes she was asked to prepare following the Clubhouse Cooks committee meeting. "What time?" Loretta asked.

"Five," Pauline said. "It's all potluck."

"Okay. Homemade bread for a crowd. Preferably rolls," Loretta said with a smile. "I think I've got it." She was about to turn back inside when she heard a loud thump against the side of the house. Standing where she was in the middle of the garage, she was unable to see what was going on, but whatever it was threw Nigel into an immediate fit.

"Nigel!" Pauline shouted. She wrangled the leash around her arm and gave it a hard yank. The dog was unfettered. He strained hard on the leash.

Loretta moved quickly to the end of the garage and stepped out to see what was going on. What she found was a large, angry cat with his face pressed against the glass in the front bedroom window. She rolled her eyes and sighed. "Calm down, Milo," she said and slapped her palm against the side of the house. A decorative flower bush prevented her from reaching the window.

"Milo? More like Monster." Pauline reached down and picked up the snarling dog in her arms and marched down the road.

Loretta shook her head and turned back to the garage. She hit the electric keypad on her way in, and the overhead door began to slide down behind her. She surveyed her kitchen and placed her hands on her hips. "Looks like I have some baking to do," she said to the cat.

Milo did not respond. He remained on vigilant watch in the bedroom window.

A few hours later, Loretta pulled the dust cover off her large stand mixer. She opened the pantry and retrieved her flour and sugar canisters. Originally, she had placed both in a cabinet close to the stove, but the pantry seemed like a more appropriate place.

From memory, Loretta began her preparation of her favorite bread recipe. She set a small saucepan on the stove and began melting a pound of butter. She added four cups of milk and watched carefully to prevent any scalding. She opened a large sack of instant yeast and measured out six tablespoons into a glass measuring cup, then added a cup of warm water and a tablespoon of sugar. She set the yeast aside and placed the remainder of the larger bag in the freezer.

Next, Loretta removed the butter and milk mixture from the stove and set it to the side to cool. She poured four cups of water into the mixer and slowly added the milk and melted butter, three teaspoons of salt, and three-quarters of a cup of sugar. She cracked four eggs and added them to the bowl, then turned on the mixer.

She waited until the mixture was successfully blended, then added the yeast, which had foamed up since she set it aside. After she poured the yeast mixture into the mixer bowl, she began adding bread flour a cup at a time. After four cups, she replaced the mixer paddle with the dough hook and added more flour. When a ball of dough formed. Loretta turned down the mixer speed and allowed the dough hook to knead the dough for several minutes until it was ready to place in a large bowl.

Two hours later, the aroma of fresh baked bread filled the entire house. Loretta carefully removed the last pan of rolls from the oven and set them on the countertop. She checked her hair one last time and then placed the still hot rolls in a large basket with the rest of them. Unlike her first trip to the clubhouse with a batch of homemade rolls, she decided to bring them along in two baskets set in the back seat of her car.

While she packed up her car, Loretta thought of little more than the discovery she had made the first time she attempted to bake enough homemade rolls for her new community of neighbors. She shuddered at the thought of returning to the same scene where she had discovered Nina's body. In the days since then, nothing much had come of the investigation. Her last conversation with Deputy Hargraves revealed that much. Still, she wondered, who would have had any reason to murder Nina? She assumed the death was a murder based on what the police had said, but honestly, she still had no idea what the truth was about anything.

A thought hit her. She froze in place and raced back inside the house to check something. If she was right, she may have just solved a murder.

CHAPTER FIFTEEN

Ten minutes later, Loretta eased her car into the last parking spot she could find behind the clubhouse. Apparently, a number of others had the idea to drive their own vehicles rather than walk. She noticed a long line of golf carts parked in front of the building as well. Maybe she could consider trading in her car for one.

With both large baskets hooked over her arms, Loretta made her way inside the clubhouse. She hesitated when she stepped inside.

"What's the matter with you?" Brigitte shouted. "Are you just going to stand there?" Loretta faced the large crowd of people. She spotted an oblong table on the other side of the room where the food had been set. She wanted to move her feet and legs and head in that direction, but her body just wouldn't work.

"Leave her alone." Pauline made a beeline for Loretta, followed closely by Kelly. "Here, let me take these from you."

"Are you alright?" Kelly asked. She placed her arm gingerly behind Loretta's back and led her through the crowd to a small table close to the kitchen door.

"I'm fine," Loretta said. "It's just that this is my first time here since I found Nina."

"Understandable." Kelly jerked her head in the direction of the food table. "It amazes me how you can bring out Pauline's good side."

"Yeah, I am not quite sure what is going on there," Loretta said. She spoke the words, but her mind was on the crowd. She scanned it for any sign of the person she was sure had killed Nina. Her eyes stopped on a familiar face, this time out of uniform. "What is the deputy doing here? Does he live here, too?"

Kelly looked around and spotted him. "He doesn't live here, but his presence is common. I'm not a bit surprised he decided to show up tonight, given the fact that we have yet to figure out who killed Nina."

Loretta turned her full attention to Kelly. She

looked in her eyes and whispered, "I think I know who did it."

"Loretta," Gwen called to her from behind. Loretta whipped her head around and stared at the woman. "You look like you've just seen a ghost."

"Maybe I have," Loretta said, a little louder than she expected. Her words caught the attention of the rest of the group. A hush fell over the large room. Deputy Hargraves made his way over.

"Is there something wrong over here?" he asked. His attempt to keep his voice down had no effect. The entire room was tuned into the scene.

Loretta sighed. This was not the way she had planned to go about it, but there she was. "Something dawned on me a little while ago," she announced. "I didn't want to believe it, but after looking over my contract and the deed to my house, I realized that I had no choice."

"I have no idea what you're going on about, but around here, we're not the type of people to make scenes in the middle of an event," Gwen scolded her.

"Are you the type of person to strike an old friend over the head and leave her to die in the middle of this room, then?" Loretta asked. She could hear the collective gasp from the people around her.

"What are you talking about?" Deputy Hargraves asked her.

"Nothing," Gwen said quickly. "Clearly, we made a mistake when we approved the purchase of her house. You may behave like this in public back home, Miss Barksdale, but around here, we don't tolerate such boorish behavior."

"You know, it wasn't clear to me for a little while what the motive might have been," Loretta said. She allowed her voice to carry across the room. "I'll admit that I still don't know why you did it. Although, I suspect it has something to do with the missing funds around the village."

"You are acting absurd," Gwen said. "Be quiet or I will press charges against you for harassment." She stared at the deputy and waited for his response.

"Now, you just hold on. I'm eager to see where this goes," Deputy Hargraves said. He folded his arms over his chest and turned back to Loretta. "What makes you think Mrs. Neville is the killer?"

"Yesterday, when you and I spoke, you told me that the sheriff's department had released very few details," she said.

"That's right," he said.

"It didn't occur to me until I was loading my car to come here, but Gwen Neville told me days ago she couldn't understand how anyone would have enough rage in their hearts to hit Nina Carpenter that hard." Her words were followed by another collective intake of air. Had the circumstances not been so serious, Loretta would have been tempted to laugh.

"You're insane," Gwen hissed. She turned to walk away but was stopped when her husband Wally stepped in front of her.

"Is it true?" Wally confronted his wife. His lower lip trembled. "Did you kill her? Did you kill my Nina?"

"Your Nina!" Gwen raged. "She was not your Nina! You are married to me, or have you forgotten that?"

She turned back to Loretta. "This is none of your business. I never confessed to a thing, but you have certainly managed to destroy my marriage in the few days you've been here."

"Can you explain why there is still a founder's fee on my contract?" Loretta asked. "Someone told me that it had been discontinued years ago after some controversy."

"I have no idea what you're talking about," Gwen said.

"I can go back home and get the contract," Loretta said. "It was signed by you less than thirty days ago."

"Is that true?" Clay emerged from the crowd. "Did you charge this woman the founder's fee?"

"Oh, so what if I did?" Gwen shouted. "It isn't like she would have known any better. Not unless someone else clued her into it."

"Either way, you probably need to come with me for now," Deputy Hargraves said. "I think you have some questions to answer."

"I am not going anywhere," Gwen yelled. "I've done nothing wrong. I did everything for this community. I found the money to do everything you people wanted to do. When you wanted new landscaping on the golf course, I made it happen. When you decided this building needed a kitchen upgrade, who found the money? Who cares where it came from? I did this for all of you!"

"Why did you hit Nina over the head then?" Loretta asked.

"Because she had it coming to her," Gwen spat back. Her face registered shock a second after the words left her mouth.

"Gwen Neville, you are under arrest for the murder of Nina Carpenter," Deputy Hargraves said. He produced a set of handcuffs and approached her.

Gwen tried to push through the crowd but was quickly stopped. She landed in Wally's arms. "Please,

Wally," she begged him. "This is not fair. You fell in love with another woman. You drove me to this."

"I doubt that was the only motive," the deputy said. "I have a feeling Nina might have discovered your creative accounting practices and confronted you about them."

"If she had just kept her nose out of it, she might still be alive," Gwen muttered.

Loretta felt her legs go weak again. She wobbled slightly on her feet. Pauline and Kelly rushed to her side as the crowd split to allow the deputy through. They guided her out of the main room and to a stool just inside the kitchen door. "Okay, now it is time for you to fess up," Pauline said. "You have to clue us in on what is going on with you."

Loretta waited until she regained her senses and shook her head. "I don't want my private business known, Pauline," she said. "Surely you can understand that."

"I am afraid she is right," Kelly said. "You really ought to tell at least a couple of people if something is going on with your health. I can assure you that Pauline will keep your secret to herself, right?"

Pauline lowered her eyes under Kelly's glare. "On my honor, I will not tell a soul," she said.

Loretta sighed again. She rested her head in her

hands for a moment. "There isn't anything wrong with my health. It's my husband that's the problem, Well, my ex-husband, anyway. He'd been lying to me for years, and our divorce was messy, to say the least."

"Is that why you chose to come here and retire so early?" Pauline asked.

Loretta nodded. "He took me for a lot of money, and I didn't handle it well at the time. My doctors told me to be cautious with stressful situations, so I thought coming here would be my best bet."

Kelly chuckled and patted her shoulder. "I would advise keeping your nose out of murder cases then."

**

If you enjoyed Death Rolls in, check out the next book in the series, Frying For Clues, today!

AUTHOR'S NOTE

I'd love to hear your thoughts on my books, the storylines, and anything else that you'd like to comment on—reader feedback is very important to me. My contact information, along with some other helpful links, is listed on the next page. If you'd like to be on my list of "folks to contact" with updates, release and sales notifications, etc.… just shoot me an email and let me know. Thanks for reading!

Also…

… if you're looking for more great reads, Summer Prescott Books publishes several popular series by outstanding Cozy Mystery authors.

CONTACT GRETCHEN ALLEN

Visit my website for more information about new releases, upcoming projects, and be sure to check out my special Members Only section for extra freebies and fun!

Website: www.gretchenallen.com

Email: contact@gretchenallen.com

Visit the Summer Prescott Books website to find even more great reads!

Made in United States
North Haven, CT
26 January 2024